Peeper
and
Zeep

Adam Gudeon

I Like to Read®

Holiday House / New York

To my parents—
Loretta and Marvin,
Arthur and Susan

I LIKE TO READ is a registered trademark of Holiday House, Inc.

Copyright © 2017 by Adam Gudeon
All Rights Reserved
HOLIDAY HOUSE is registered in the U.S. Patent and Trademark Office.
Printed and Bound in November 2016 at Tien Wah Press, Johor Bahru, Johor, Malaysia.
The artwork was created with ink and digital coloring.
www.holidayhouse.com
First Edition
1 3 5 7 9 10 8 6 4 2

Library of Congress Cataloging-in-Publication Data
Names: Gudeon, Adam, author.
Title: Peeper and Zeep / Adam Gudeon.
Description: First edition. | New York : Holiday House, [2017] | Series: I
like to read | Summary: "Peeper, a chick who has injured his wing, and
Zeep, an alien who has crashed his spaceship, hope Frog, an inventor can
help them return to their homes"— Provided by publisher.
Identifiers: LCCN 2016004120 | ISBN 9780823436743 (hardcover)
Subjects: | CYAC: Chickens—Fiction. | Animals—Infancy—Fiction. |
Extraterrestrial beings—Fiction. | Frogs—Fiction. | Helpfulness—Fiction. |
Classification: LCC PZ7.G93495 Pe 2017 | DDC [E]—dc23 LC record available at
https://lccn.loc.gov/2016004120

ISBN 978-0-8234-3779-5 (paperback)

This is Peeper.

This is Zeep.

Peeper fell.

He broke his wing.

Zeep fell. He broke his spaceship.

Peeper is lost.

Zeep is lost.

Peeper and Zeep meet.

How will Peeper get home?
How will Zeep get home?

Can Frog help?

Peeper and Zeep go up.

Peeper and Zeep go down.

Frog will try again.

Peeper and Zeep go up.

They go and go.

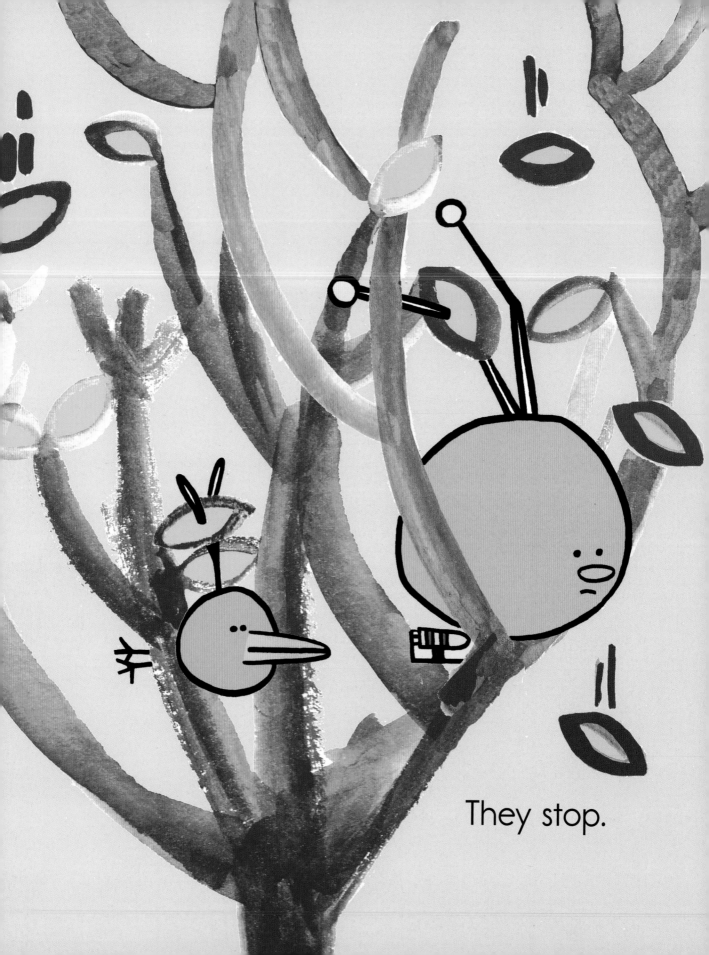

They stop.

Frog must try again.

Peeper, Zeep
and Frog
rest first.

Now they all try.

Now they all work.

Peeper and Zeep have a nice new home.
They wait.

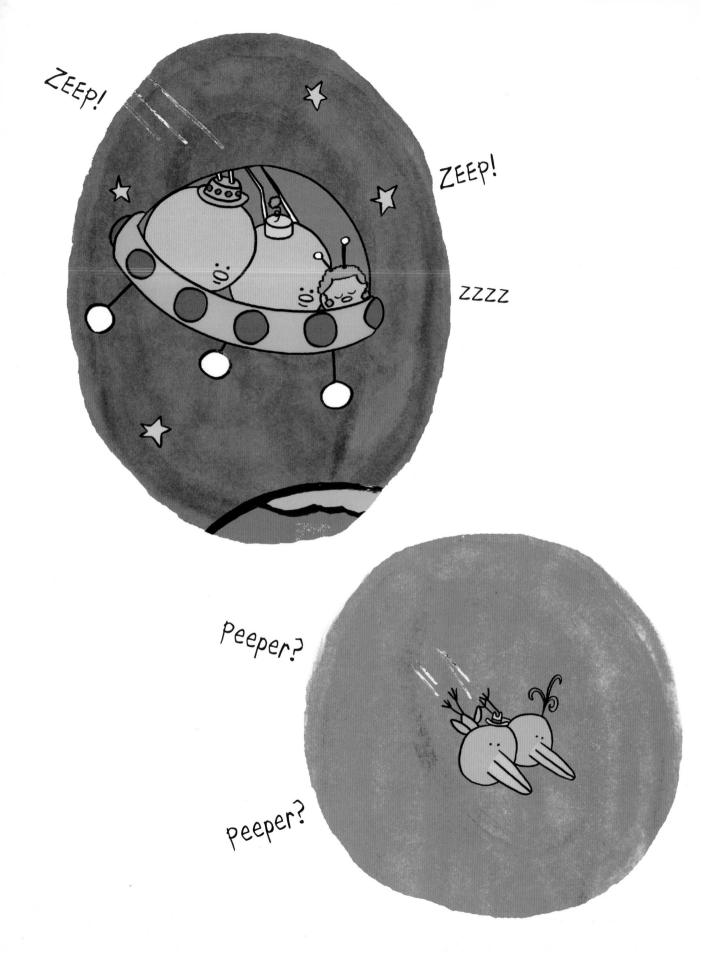